Dear Parent:
Your child's lov ts here!

Every child learns to read or her own speed.
You can help your young ...ome more confident
by encouraging his ... can also guide
your child's spiritua biblical values
and Bible stories, li nderkidz. From
books your child re e reads alone,
there are I Can Rec

SHARED READING

Basic language, word repetition, and whimsical
illustrations, ideal for sharing with your emergent reader.

BEGINNING READING

Short sentences, familiar words, and simple concepts for
children eager to read on their own.

READING WITH HELP

Engaging stories, longer sentences, and language play
for developing readers.

READING ALONE

Complex plots, challenging vocabulary, and high-interest
topics for the independent reader.

ADVANCED READING

Short paragraphs, chapters, and exciting themes for the
perfect bridge to chapter books.

I Can Read! books have introduced children to the joy of reading since
1957. Featuring award-winning authors and illustrators and a fabulous
cast of beloved characters, I Can Read! books set the standard for
beginning readers.

JUL 2010

A lifetime of discovery begins with the magical words **"I Can Read!"**

Visit www.icanread.com for information on enriching your child's reading experience.
Visit www.zonderkidz.com for more Zonderkidz I Can Read! titles.

Turn all your worries over to [God].
He cares about you.
—*1 Peter 5:7*

ZONDERKIDZ

Frank and Beans and the Scary Campout
Copyright © 2010 by Kathy-jo Wargin
Illustrations © 2010 by Anthony Lewis

Requests for information should be addressed to:

Zondervan, *Grand Rapids, Michigan 49530*

Library of Congress Cataloging-in-Publication Data

Wargin, Kathy-jo.
    Frank and Beans and the scary campout / story by Kathy-jo Wargin ;
pictures by Anthony Lewis.
        p. cm.
    Summary: While camping with his dog Beans, Frank begins to hear scary
sounds that make him question whether or not he should go back into the house.
    ISBN 978-0-310-71850-5 (softcover)
    [1. Camping—Fiction. 2. Fear—Fiction. 3. Dogs—Fiction. 4. Christian life—
Fiction.] I. Lewis, Anthony, 1966- ill. II. Title.
PZ7.W234Fr 2010
[E]—dc22
{B}   2009003012

Editor: Mary Hassinger
Art direction: Jody Langley

Printed in China

10 11 12 13 14 15 /SCC/ 6 5 4 3 2 1

Frank and Beans
and the
Scary Campout

story by Kathy-jo Wargin

pictures by Anthony Lewis

Frank tested the tent zipper.

"I think it will be fine, Beans,"

he said.

Frank had camped many times.

He always camped with his mom,

dad, and little sister, Birdie.

Tonight, just Frank and Beans
would sleep in the yard.
"Ready for the big campout?"
asked Frank's dad.
"Night will be here soon."

Dad gave Frank a flashlight.

He gave Frank books

and a bag of popcorn.

Dad reached to pet Beans.

Beans was not there.

He was busy trying to get popcorn.

It spilled all over the lawn.

Soon it was dark.

Frank and Beans went into the tent.

Frank snuggled in his sleeping bag.

He turned on the flashlight.

He opened a book.

It was a quiet night.

Beans was cozy and sleepy.

Crick-crick-crick.

Frank looked at Beans

Crick-crick-crick.

Beans moved closer to Frank.

"Shhh. Do you hear that?"

Frank asked Beans.

Crick-crick-crick.

Frank worried about the sound.

Was it a branch in the wind?

Was it a frog? A bird?

Then came more sounds.

Hoo-hoo-hoo.

What was the crick sound?

What was the hoo sound?

Frank wanted to unzip the tent.

He wanted to look outside.

Frank was afraid. So was Beans.

Then there was another sound.

Crunch-crunch-crunch.

"Beans, I hear CRUNCHING,"

Frank whispered.

Beans heard it too.

Crunch-crunch-crunch.

Beans growled.

The noise stopped.

Beans stopped growling.

The noise started.

"This was a bad idea, Beans.

I do not like camping alone,"

said Frank.

Frank wanted to go inside.

He began to unzip the tent.

Beans jumped out!

Frank was surprised.

He zipped the tent shut and sat up.

Beans was gone.

Frank was very worried.

What if the monster ate Beans?

What if the monster ate HIM?

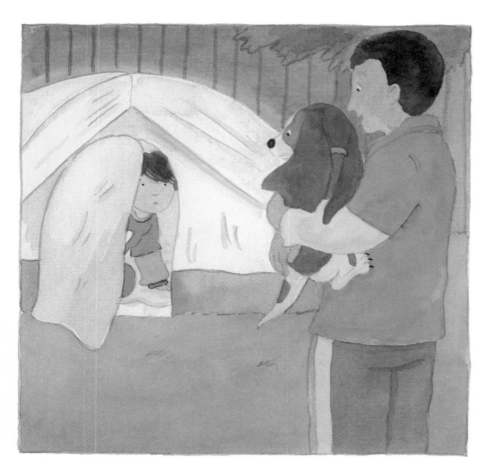

Then Frank's dad came to the tent.

He had Beans.

"Beans came to the house,"

he said.

"Is everything okay?"

Frank began to cry.

He told his dad about the

crick-crick-crick.

"That was a grasshopper.

They sing at night," his dad said.

Frank told about the hoo-hoo-hoo.

"That was an owl.

He was resting in a tree," said Dad.

Then Frank told about the crunching!

Just then, Beans ran away.

Frank and his dad followed.

"Here is your crunching monster,"

said Frank's dad.

There sat a fat raccoon.

It was eating the spilled popcorn.

Frank and his dad laughed.

Then Frank said, "I was scared.

It was hard to be alone."

"You were not alone, Frank,"
Dad said.

"Yes I was. Beans ran away,"
said Frank.

"Frank, who watches over

grasshoppers?" Frank's dad asked.

Frank thought about this.

He answered, "God."

"And who watches over owls?"

"God," said Frank.

"And who watches over raccoons?"

"God does that too," Frank smiled.

"And who watches over you?" asked Frank's dad.

"God does!" he answered.

"Right! You are never alone.

God is always with you," said Dad.

"Even in a tent by yourself."

Frank listened to the night sounds.

They sounded nice.

Frank climbed into the tent.

Beans and Frank's dad went in too.

In the glow of the flashlight,

all three ate handfuls of popcorn.

Crunch-crunch-crunch.

Frank was happy.

It was going to be a noisy night.